D1487636

Alfred A. Knopf New York

BIG, BIGGER, BIGGEST

Adventure

written by **KATE BANKS**

illustrated by **PAUL YALOWITZ**

THIS IS A BORZOI BOOK
PUBLISHED BY ALFRED A. KNOPF, INC.

Text copyright © 1990 by Katherine Anne Banks
Illustrations copyright © 1990 by Paul Yalowitz
All rights reserved under International and Pan-American Copyright
Conventions. Published in the United States by Alfred A. Knopf, Inc.,
New York, and simultaneously in Canada by Random House of Canada
Limited, Toronto. Distributed by Random House, Inc., New York.
Book design by Elizabeth Hardie
Manufactured in Singapore

2   4   6   8   10   9   7   5   3   1

Library of Congress Cataloging-in-Publication Data:
Banks, Kate, 1960—
Big, bigger, biggest adventure / Kate Banks ;
illustrated by Paul Yalowitz. p.   cm.
Summary: One mishap follows another
when three large brothers take a bicycle trip.
ISBN 0-394-89857-5. ISBN 0-394-99857-X (lib. bdg.)
[1. Brothers—Fiction.   2. Bicycles and bicycling—Fiction.
3. Size—Fiction.]   I. Yalowitz, Paul, ill.
II. Title. PZ7.B22594Bi   1990   [E]—dc20 89-34919 CIP AC

For my brother Philip
and my sisters
Amy and Nancy

K. B.

For my sister Lynn
and my brothers Eric and Stuart
—may we be children forever

P. Y.

Once there were three brothers.
Here they are.

Peter,   Louis,   and Henry.

One fine morning Peter said, "Let's go for a bicycle ride."
"Yes," said Louis. "A nice long one."
"And let's not forget lunch," said Henry.
So the three brothers packed a picnic and off they pedaled.

Soon they came to a tall mountain.
Beyond it was an even taller mountain.
And beyond that was the tallest mountain of all.
"We can do it," they said as they started up the
tallest mountain of all.

They had not gone far when
Peter, who was rather fat,
said, "My, this is hard!"

Louis, who was even fatter
than Peter, said, "It is even
harder for me."

And Henry, who was the fattest
of the three brothers, said,
"But it is hardest of all for me."

At last they reached the top, puffing and panting.
"I am hungry," said Peter. "Let's have lunch."
"Where shall we eat?" said Louis.
"Right here," said Henry, who was standing on a
nice green patch of grass.

The three brothers plopped themselves
down. But they were not very careful.
Peter sat right on top of an angry
bumblebee. "Ouch!" he cried.
Louis sat on top of an even angrier
bumblebee. "Ouch! Ouch!" he cried.
And Henry sat on top of the
angriest bumblebee of all. "Ouch! Ouch!
Ouch!" he cried.

The three brothers jumped into the air
and onto their bicycles.

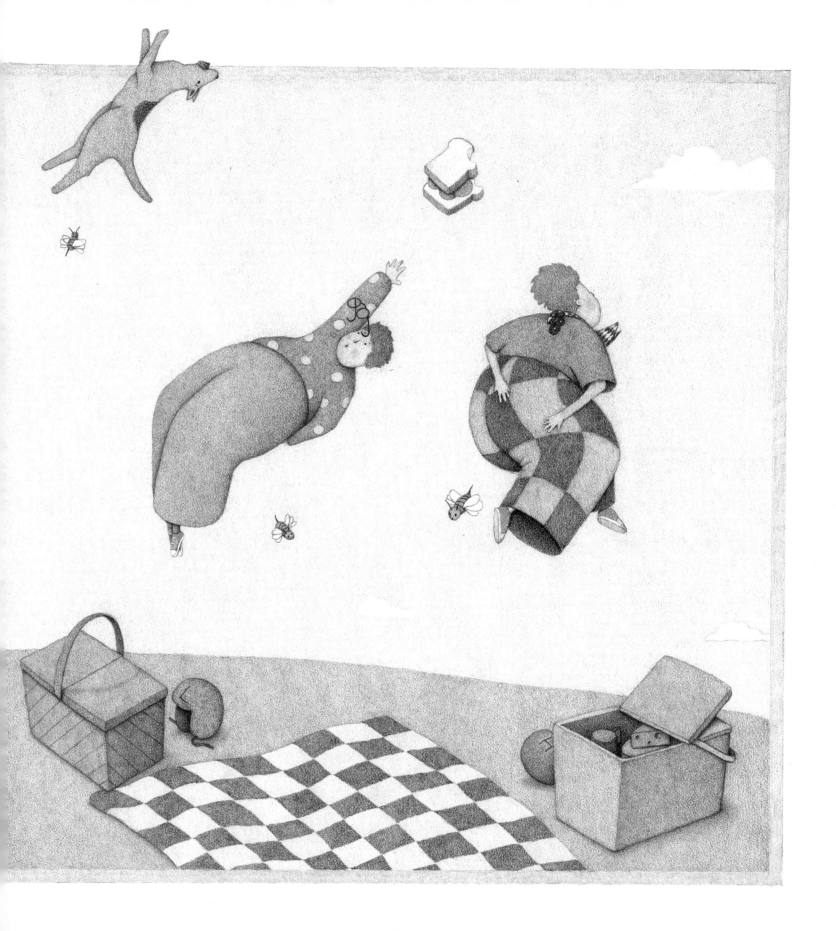

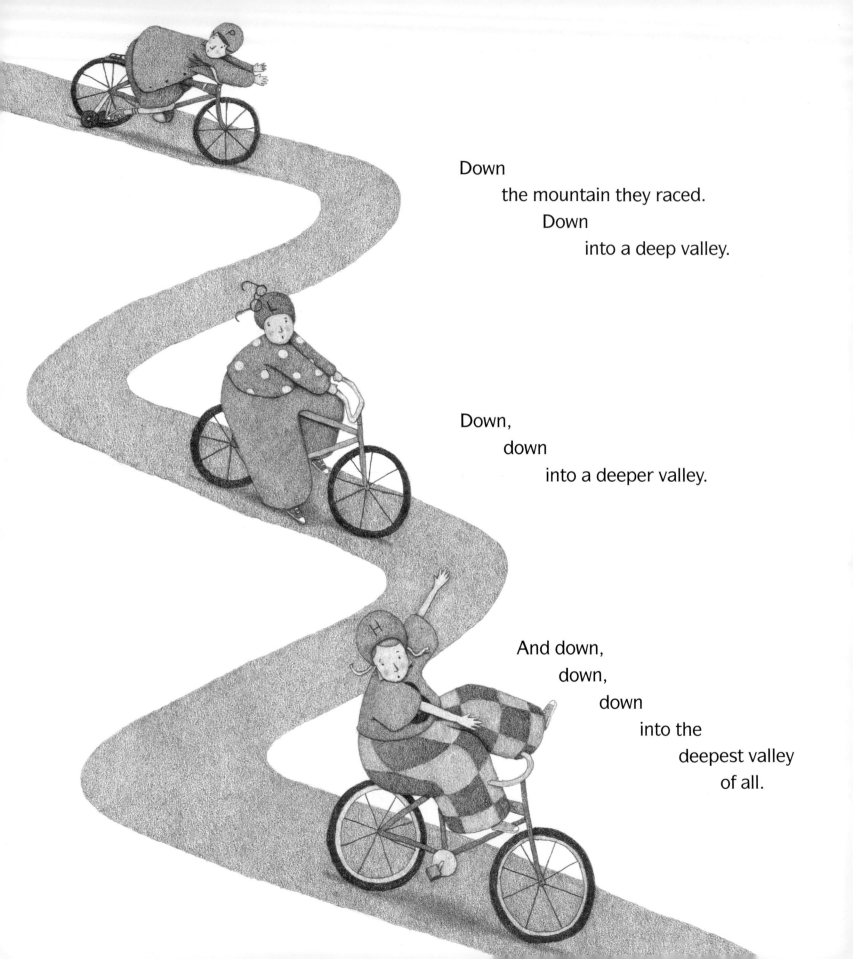

Down
    the mountain they raced.
        Down
            into a deep valley.

Down,
    down
        into a deeper valley.

And down,
    down,
        down
            into the
                deepest valley
                    of all.

"Look!" said Peter as they reached the bottom.
The sky was growing black.

A dark cloud settled over Peter's head.
An even darker cloud settled over
Louis's head.
And the darkest cloud of all settled over
Henry's head.

Henry began to pedal fast.
Louis pedaled even faster than Henry.
And Peter pedaled the fastest of all.
But they could not escape the clouds.
Down came the rain.

"Oh no," said Peter when
the rain had stopped.
"I am wet from head to toe."

"But look at me,"
said Henry.
"I am wettest of all."

"I am wetter than you,"
said Louis.

The three brothers wrung themselves out.

Then they pedaled into the bright sunshine.
Onto a country road and past a little farmhouse.
They waved to some snorting pigs and a crowing rooster
sitting on an open gate.
Suddenly Peter shouted, "Stop!"
But it was too late.

Three fat cows raced through the gate
and ran headfirst into the three brothers.
What a mess they made!
Cows and bicycles all over the road.
The cows mooing.
And the three brothers moaning and
groaning.
"Ohh," sighed Peter, who had a big
bump on his head.
"Ahhh," sighed Louis, who had an even
bigger bump on his head.
And "Ooooh," sighed Henry, who had
the biggest bump of all.

"We are lucky that our bicycles are in one
piece," said Peter as the three brothers
picked themselves up.
They helped the cows to their feet.

And on they pedaled out of the countryside, into a bustling city, and up to the entrance of a park.

A big sign read NO BICYCLES ALLOWED!
But the three brothers did not see it.

They kept right on pedaling.
They waved at the dog-walkers and the children playing and at three stern policemen, who did not wave back.
The first policeman shook his head at Peter. "Didn't you read the sign?" he called in a loud voice.
The second policeman shook his fist at Louis. "No bicycles in the park!!" he called in an even louder voice.
The third policeman stomped his foot at Henry. "You are breaking the law!!!" he shouted in the loudest voice of all.
"Get out of here as fast as you can!"

"We are very sorry," said the three brothers.
And off they pedaled, as fast as they could,

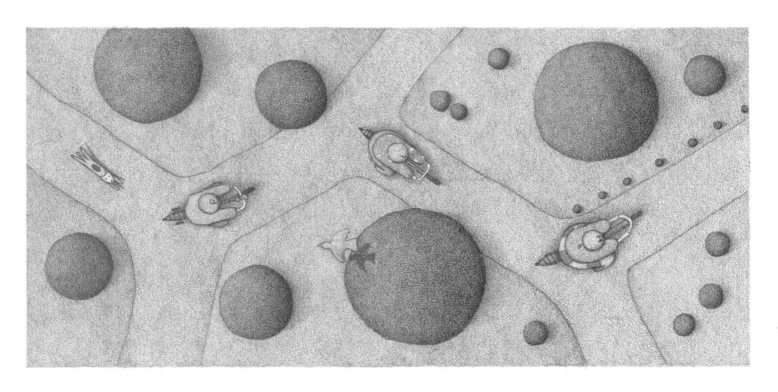

turning left,   turning right,   then left again

until they had reached the far end of the park.
Then the three brothers stopped.

Peter wanted to turn one way.

Henry wanted to turn the other.

Louis was left to decide. "Let's go straight," he said.

"Where are we?" said Peter.

"I'm sure I don't know," said Louis.

"We are lost," said Henry, who was exactly right.

So the three brothers pedaled
straight on.
Bump! went Peter over a wide ditch.
Bump! Bump! went Louis over a wider
ditch.
Bump! Bump! Bump! went Henry
over the widest ditch of all.

Now the three brothers were really in trouble.

Peter had a flat tire.   Louis's tire was even   And poor Henry's tire
                                flatter than Peter's.   was the flattest of all.

"What will we do?" moaned Peter.
"We'll never get home," wailed Louis.
"But look!" said Henry, who was beginning to smile.
Beyond a dirt road, in back of a small hill, and not
too far away was a rooftop that looked very familiar.

On the three brothers wobbled,
as quickly as they dared,
down the dirt road,
over the small hill,
and up the driveway
to their own front door.

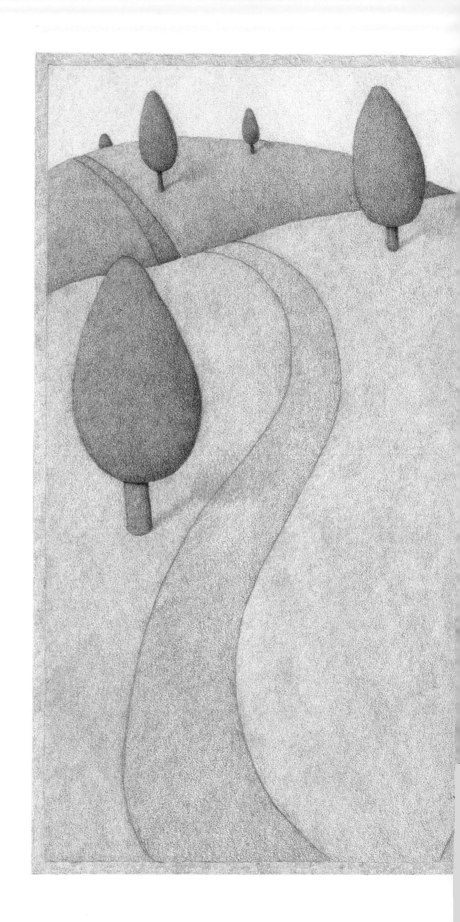

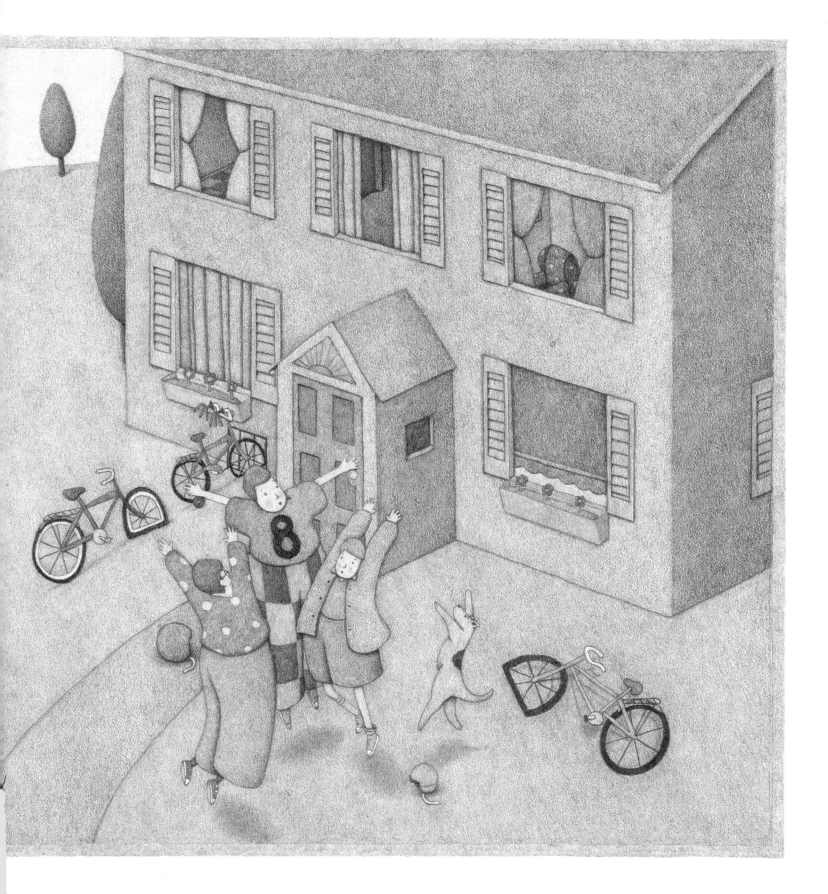

What a day it had been for the three brothers!
"I," said Peter, "am happy to be home."
"But I," said Louis, "am even happier than you."
"And I," said Henry, "am the happiest of all!"